and the
BIG BAD
WOLF

For Reuben
R.I.

For Finley and Fred
K.M.

ORCHARD BOOKS

First published in Great Britain in 2016 by The Watts Publishing Group

1 3 5 7 9 10 8 6 4 2

Text © Rose Impey 2016

Illustrations © Katharine McEwen 2016

The moral rights of the author and illustrator have been asserted.

A CIP catalogue record for this book is available from the British Library.

ISBN 978 1 40832 520 9 (HB)
ISBN 978 1 40832 526 1 (PB)

Printed in China

MIX
Paper from
responsible sources
FSC
www.fsc.org
FSC® C104740

The paper and board used in this book are made from wood from responsible sources

Orchard Books
An imprint of Hachette Children's Group
Part of The Watts Publishing Group Limited
Carmelite House, 50 Victoria Embankment, London EC4Y 0DZ

An Hachette UK Company
www.hachette.co.uk
www.hachettechildrens.co.uk

and the
BIG BAD
WOLF

Rose Impey · Katharine McEwen

ORCHARD

Cast of Characters

Sir Lance-a-Little

Harold the Horse

Princess Plum

Huffalot the Dragon

The Big, Bad Wolf

Sir Lance-a-Little looked out of
his castle window and cheered,
"Hurrah!"
There was a new challenge from
the dragon.

He set off *immediately* on his trusty horse, Harold, to meet and *defeat* his No. 1 enemy: Huffalot!

Sir Lance-a-Little was the bravest and cleverest knight in the whole kingdom of Notalot.

Or that was what he liked to think.

Just then, Sir Lance-a-Little's cousin, Princess Plum, saw the message and set off, too. If there was a fight, Princess Plum didn't want to miss it.

Annoyingly, she didn't have a
horse. So she ran, as fast as she
could, to catch up with him.
She ran …

... straight into a Big, Bad Wolf.
"And where are you going to in such a hurry?" asked the wolf.

"To see a fight," puffed Princess Plum. "And I don't want to be late."

"Perhaps I could
show you a short cut,"
the wolf offered, smiling.
A short cut was just what
Princess Plum needed.
She followed the wolf deep into
the wood, which really wasn't
a good idea!

Meanwhile, in his cave, the dragon was filing his teeth ... And sharpening his claws ... preparing to meet his No. 1 enemy, Sir Lance-a-Little.

Huffalot was the fiercest and the most cunning dragon in the whole of Notalot.

He was also the most handsome! Or that was what *he* liked to think.

As Sir Lance-a-Little rode along, he imagined Huffalot cowering in his cave. He could almost hear the dragon's tail rattling in fear.

But, suddenly, Sir Lance-a-Little heard something quite different.

It was the voice of his pestiferous cousin, Princess Plum!

"You're not putting me in a pot," she told the Big, Bad Wolf. "Watch me," replied the wolf, grinning.

Sir Lance-a-Little almost rode on
to meet the dragon. But he was
a knight of honour, after all.
First, he must save his annoying
little cousin.

Sir Lance-a-Little waved his sword
and charged into the clearing.
"Be afraid," he told the
wolf, bravely.

But the wolf didn't seem a bit
afraid. In fact, he folded his
paws and yawned!

Sir Lance-a-Little was hopping mad. He rushed forward to teach that wolf a lesson!

But the wolf was surprisingly fast on his paws. He leapt sideways.

Sir Lance-a-Little charged again.
This time the sneaky wolf stuck
out a foot and tripped him up!

And then, can you believe it, the
wolf did an even sneakier thing!

He sat on the little knight, pinning him to the ground!

"That's not fair!" Sir Lance-a-Little cried. He knew the Knights' Code of Honour off by heart, and sitting on people definitely wasn't in it!

But the wolf didn't care about honour, he only cared about his stomach.

While the wolf waited for the water to boil, Sir Lance-a-Little and his tiresome cousin glared at one another.

Suddenly, there was a roaring sound. "What's that?" asked the wolf, nervously.

"That," said Sir Lance-a-Little, "is Huffalot, the fiercest dragon in the whole of Notalot. He is famous for his colossal appetite for eating people."

23

"And wolves!" added
Princess Plum.
"Oh, yes, especially
wolves," agreed
Sir Lance-a-Little.

The wolf looked even
more nervous now.

A large head appeared
through the trees,
breathing fire.

When Huffalot saw the wolf sitting

on his No. 1 enemy, he stretched to

his full height and he ...

ROARED!

"Help! Save me!" howled the wolf, racing off with the end of his tail on fire.

Sir Lance-a-Little quickly struggled to his feet. He didn't want that dragon to think he might need rescuing. "Ready when you are!" he told Huffalot, bravely.

Sir Lance-a-Little wasn't actually
ready. He was tired out. That wolf
had weighed a ton.
Huffalot wasn't ready either.
He'd used up all his fire on that
pesky wolf.

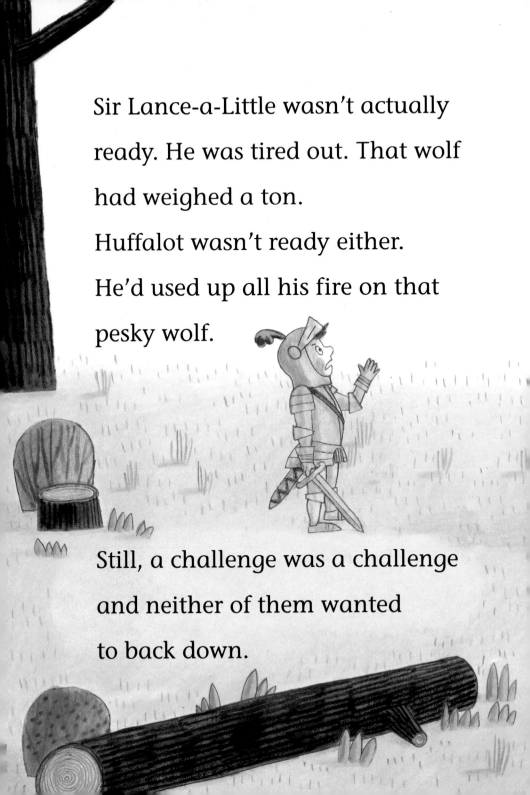

Still, a challenge was a challenge
and neither of them wanted
to back down.

But Princess Plum was hungry by now, and sick of waiting to be freed.

"Oh, bother, bother. Can't it wait till tomorrow?" she said.

Sir Lance-a-Little and Huffalot
were secretly quite happy to
put off their battle.

"I could easily have escaped, you know," Sir Lance-a-Little told Princess Plum, who nodded wisely. Wolves … dragons … It was all in a day's work for a brave little knight like him.

THE
END

Join the bravest knight in Notalot
for all his adventures!

Written by Rose Impey • Illustrated by Katharine McEwen

Orchard Books are available from all good bookshops, or can be ordered from our website:
www.orchardbooks.co.uk
or telephone 01235 400400, or fax 01235 400454.

Prices and availability are subject to change.